Printed in Italy

Published 1984 by Derrydale Books,
distributed by Crown Publishers, Inc.

ISBN : 0-517-462419

h g f e d c b a

The Three

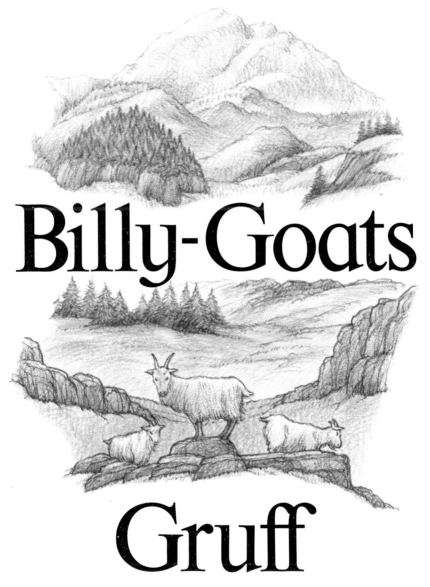

Billy-Goats

Gruff

Illustrated by Graham Percy

DERRYDALE BOOKS
New York

Once upon a time there were
three goats. They were
brothers and they were known
as the three Billy Goats Gruff.

One day, they decided to
go up the hillside to
eat the fresh green grass.

To get up the hill
they had to cross a little
stone bridge, over a rushing stream.

Now under that bridge lived a great ugly troll with eyes as big as saucers and a nose as long as a poker.

The first to cross the bridge was the youngest
Billy Goat Gruff.

Trip, trap, trip, trap, went his hooves.

"Who's that trip-trapping across my bridge?" growled the troll.

"It's me, the smallest Billy Goat Gruff," he
said in his tiny voice. "I'm going up the hillside
to eat the fresh green grass."

"Well I'm a troll-foll-de-roll,
and I'm going to eat you for
my supper!" said the troll.

"Oh, no! Don't eat me," said the little
goat. "I'm too small. Just wait
until my brother comes.
He's much bigger."

"Well be off with you then," said the troll.

A few moments mater, the second Billy Goat
Gruff reached the bridge.

Trip, trap
trip, trap,
went his hooves.

"Who's that trip-trapping across my bridge?"
growled the troll.

"It's me, the second
Billy Goat Gruff," he said in
his medium-sized voice.
"I'm going up the hillside
to eat the fresh green grass."

"Well I'm a troll-foll-de-roll,
and I'm going to eat you for
my supper!" said the troll.

"Oh no! Don't eat me.
Wait until my brother comes.
He's much bigger."

"Well be off with
you then," said
the troll.

A few moments later, the biggest
Billy Goat Gruff reached the bridge.

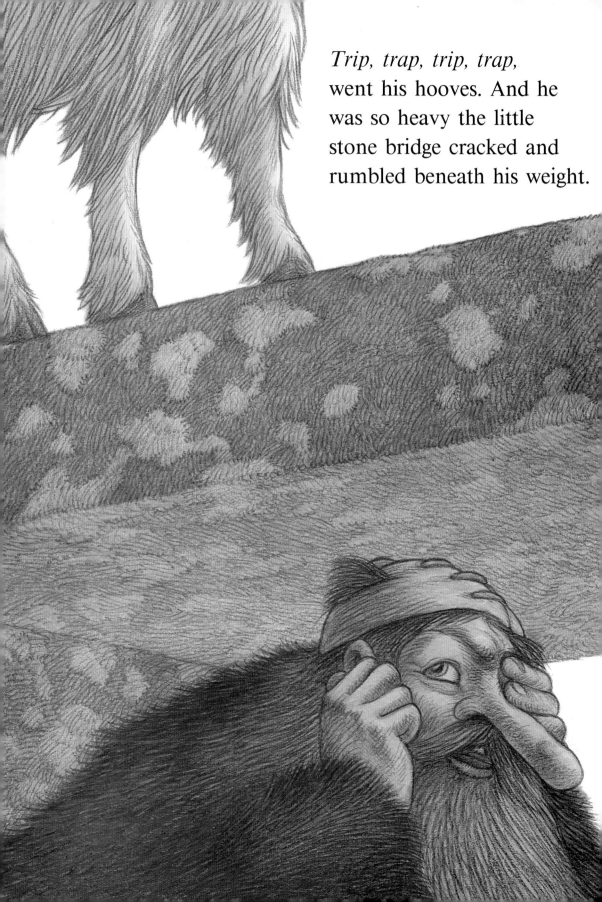

Trip, trap, trip, trap, went his hooves. And he was so heavy the little stone bridge cracked and rumbled beneath his weight.

"Who's that trip-
trapping across my bridge?"
growled the troll.

"It's me, the great Billy Goat Gruff,"
he said in his strong voice. "I'm going to
the hillside to eat the fresh green grass."

"Well I'm a troll-
foll-de-roll, and
I'm going to eat
you for my supper,"
roared the troll.

But the biggest Billy Goat Gruff roared back,
"Well come along! I've got two spears
and I'll poke your eyeballs out trough yours ears.
Besides, I've got four hooves like stones,
and I'll crush you to bits, body and bones!"
And he rushed at the troll,

and tossed
   him down
      into the
         rushing stream.

After that he went up to
the hillside to join the other
Billy Goats Gruff. They all ate
so much, and got so fat, that they
could hardly walk home again.